Hello
This book belongs to:

For Ivy, Delilah, Coco and Mabel

(And thanks to the Mitchell Guinea Pigs for the inspiration!)

HODDER CHILDREN'S BOOKS

First published in Great Britain in 2022
by Hodder and Stoughton

1 3 5 7 9 10 8 6 4 2


A CIP catalogue record for this book
is available from the British Library.

HB ISBN 978 1 444 95210 0
PB ISBN 978 1 444 95211 7

Printed and bound in China

Hodder Children's Books
An imprint of Hachette Children's Group
Part of Hodder and Stoughton
Carmelite House, 50 Victoria Embankment,
London, EC4Y 0DZ

An Hachette UK Company
www.hachette.co.uk
www.hachettechildrens.co.uk

Hodder
Children's
Books

It was a quiet Wednesday afternoon down at Pat's Pets. Pat had closed early for the day, so all the animals were hanging out and having fun.

Sid the Snake was making plans for dinner . . .

**Hey guys, are you free for a bite later?**

**Er, thanks Sid, but it's our mac and cheese night – rain check?**

The rabbits,
Ross and Rachel,
were enjoying
a game of snap . . .

And Trevor the Tortoise was
catching up on the football!

WHAT
A GOAL!

Meanwhile, in the Piggy Palace, the guinea pigs were busy doing their favourite thing: making themselves look

# FAB-U-LOUS!

They **PAMPERED** and **PREENED,**
they **BRUSHED** and **BUFFED.**

You see, all the guinea pigs just
loved looking their best!

All except **ONE.**

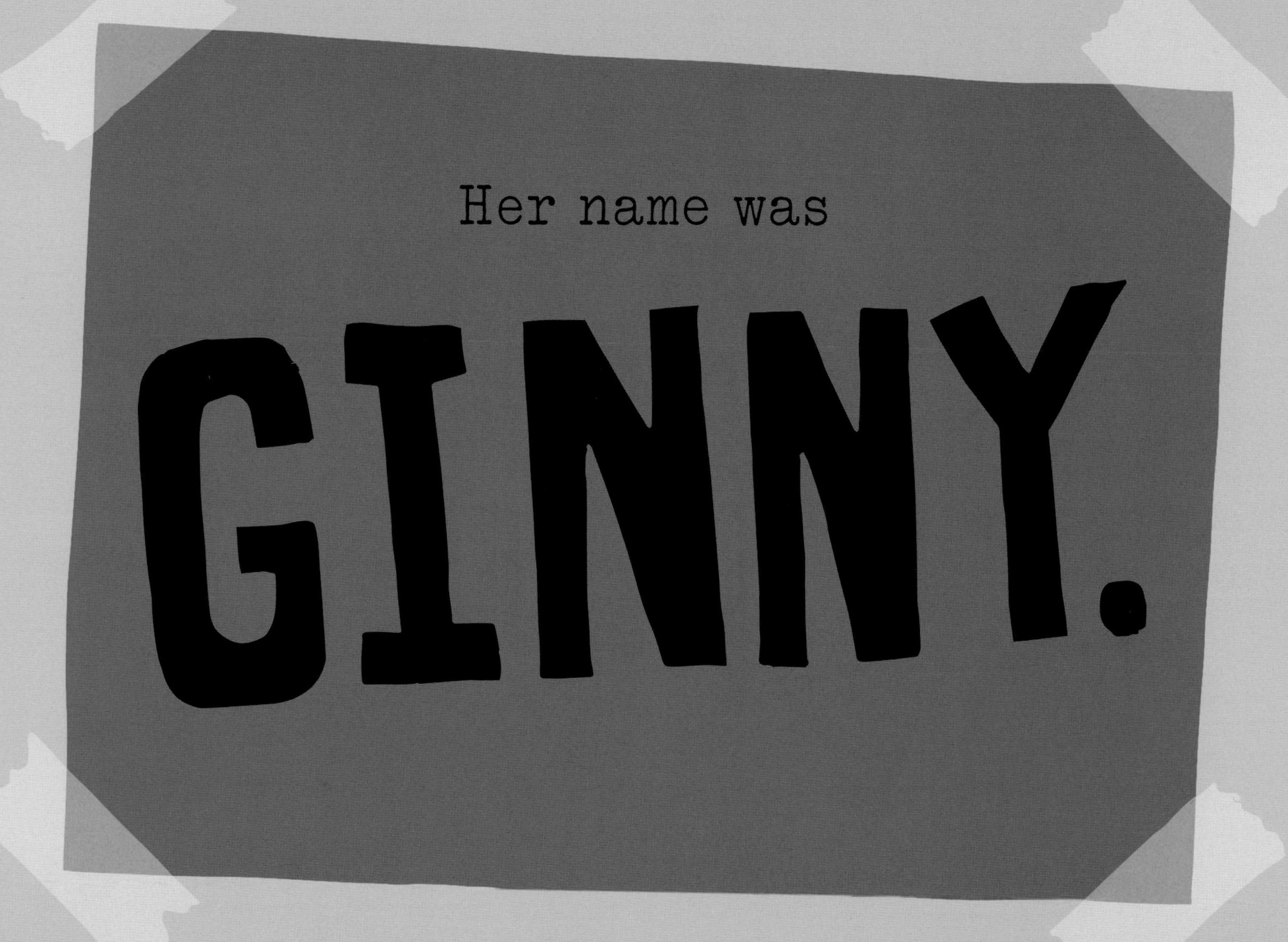


Ginny wasn't like the other guinea pigs.
She was very **SCRUFFY** and just a bit wild!

Ginny just wasn't interested in perms or pampering.
She liked running, climbing and generally mucking around.

Ginny had tried to fit in. She even asked her friend Gloria to give her a makeover.

Gloria was happy to help, though she thought Ginny was perfect.

She **PAMPERED**

**WHIRR!**

and **PREENED.**

But makeovers just weren't Ginny's style.

**"I need to find a home that's a bit more ME,"** thought Ginny.

Then, one evening, she saw something in the newspaper as she was cleaning out her home.

The animals in the picture were scruffy and messy just like she was!

**"That's where I need to go!"** she said, and started planning her escape.

In the end, the answer was right under her toes.

Ginny decided to **TUNNEL** her way out!

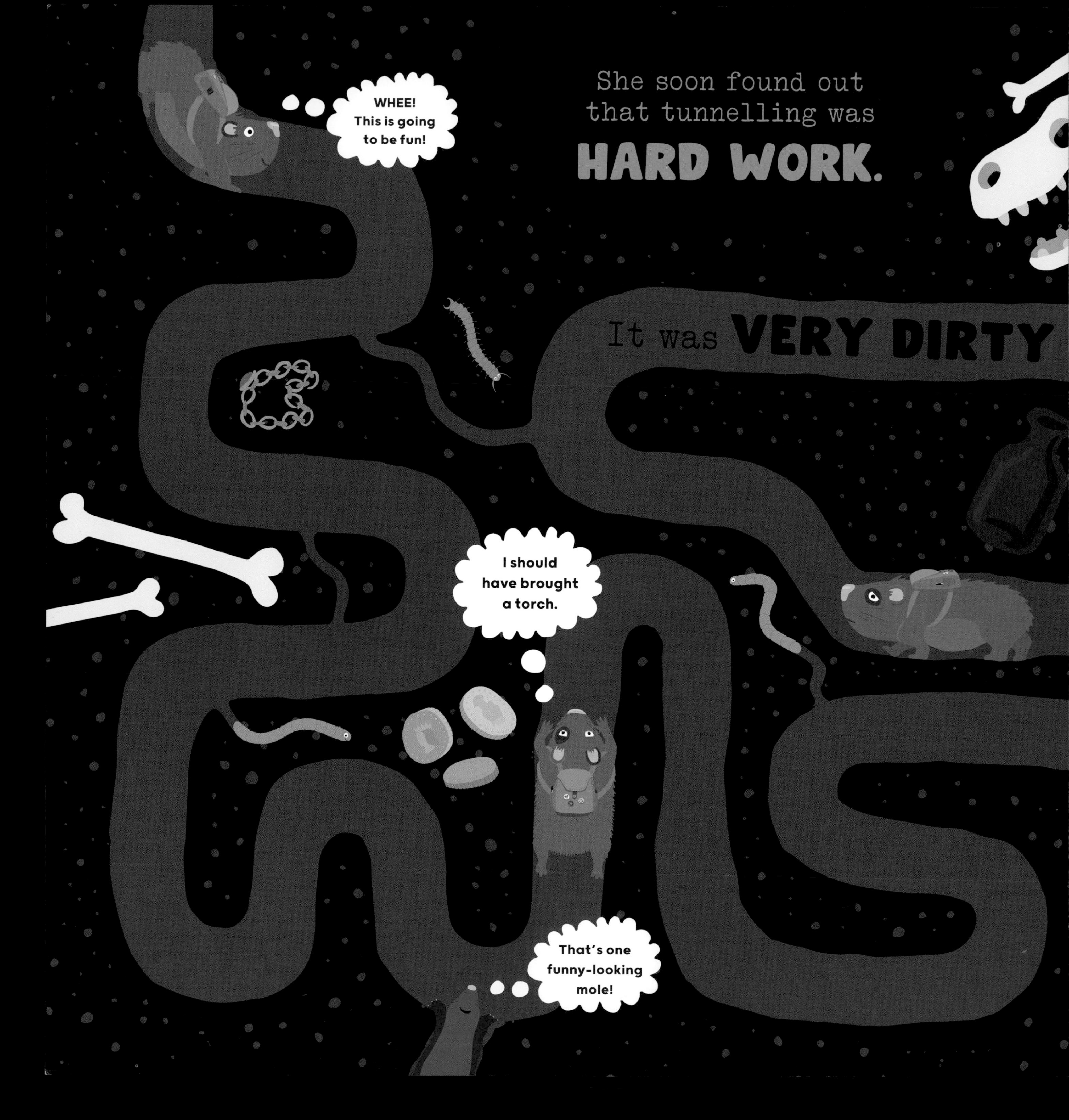
WHEE! This is going to be fun!
She soon found out that tunnelling was
HARD WORK.
It was VERY DIRTY
I should have brought a torch.
That's one funny-looking mole!

and **VERY DARK**.

Before long, Ginny was

**LOST!**

When she finally surfaced, messier than ever, she couldn't believe her eyes!

**"Am I in ANTARCTICA?"**

she asked a penguin.

**No dear, you're at THE ZOO!**

Ginny looked at all the smartly dressed penguins around her.

The babies were **FLUFFY** but not **SCRUFFY.** This wasn't the home for Ginny.

She said goodbye and disappeared back into the ice!

PENGUIN ISLAND

Ginny tunnelled for ages until her head popped up into daylight again.

# ROAR!

**"EEK! Have I dug all the way back to the prehistoric past?"**

# PHEW!

It was just a toy shop. Ginny looked at the shiny dinosaurs all in a row.

They still looked pretty scary! This place definitely wasn't the home for Ginny.

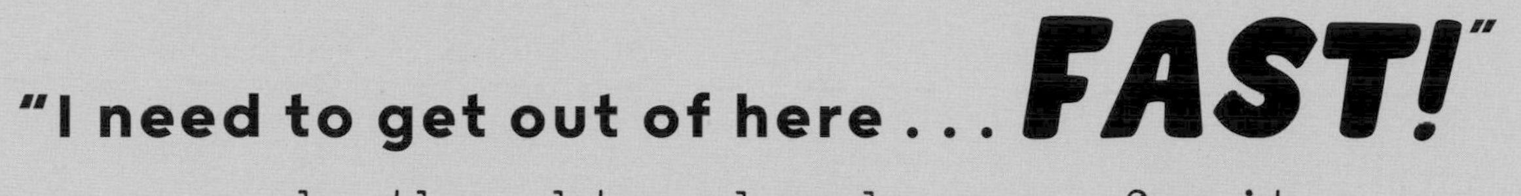


she thought, and made a run for it.

She soon spotted
the perfect

**PIG-MOBILE**

for a speedy
getaway.

It felt good
to feel the wind
in her wild fur!

For the first time
on her adventure, Ginny
was having **FUN!**

But it didn't
last long . . .

**BEEEEP!**

Ginny didn't see the kerb through her messy hair and sunglasses.

She flew through the air like a furry blur . . .

**OOPS!**

And grabbed the first
thing she could find
to slow herself down.

SNAP!

But to her
surprise
she went

UP!

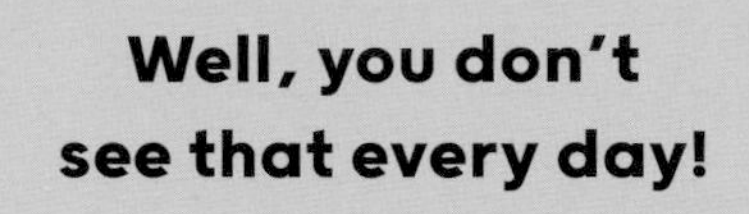


# WHAT A VIEW!

This was much better than burrowing underground. Ginny could finally see the beautiful countryside she had longed to find.

She was just
wondering how
to get down
when . . .

POP!

!?
Luckily, with
a bit of help . . .
Thank Ewe!
BOING!
Ginny landed
safely . . .
SPLAT!

She opened her eyes and smiled.
Friendly faces had gathered round
to see who had dropped in . . .

They were all as scruffy as she was! At last,

**GINNY FELT RIGHT AT HOME!**

Dear Gloria,
Wish you were here!
It's great fun in the country.
I've made lots of lovely
friends and there's
lots of fresh air.
(although it's a bit smelly!)
Please come and visit soon.
(Maybe take the bus!)
Lots of love
Ginny
X
PIGGY POST · PIGGY POST ·
50
Gloria Guinea Pig
c/o PAT'S PETS
101 Dalmation Road
The Big City
I'M ON MY WAY DARLING!
GV